This book belongs to:

_____

It's a Big World, Little Pig!

KRISTI YAMAGUCHI
Illustrated by Tim Bowers

sourcebooks
jabberwocky

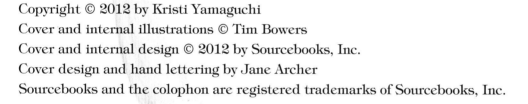

Published by Sourcebooks Jabberwocky, an imprint of Sourcebooks, Inc.
P.O. Box 4410, Naperville, Illinois 60567-4410
(630) 961-3900
Fax: (630) 961-2168
www.jabberwockykids.com

Library of Congress Cataloging-in-Publication data is on file with the publisher.

Source of Production: Lehigh Phoenix, Rockaway, New Jersey, USA
Date of Production: January 2012
Run Number: 16641

Printed and bound in the United States of America.
PX 10 9 8 7 6 5 4 3 2 1

Poppy was a pig who dreamed big.

She dreamed of being an ice-skating

star and then she made it happen!

She was star of the rink!

One day Poppy received a beautiful

invitation in the mail.

"Reach for the stars, little pig!" it read.

"Fly to Paris, France, and compete

in the World Games!"

Paris was far away from Poppy's home in New Pork City.

Poppy was excited to see new places, but she was scared
about being so far from home.

"Dream big, pig!"
exclaimed Poppy's
best friend, Emma.

"You go, girl!"
said Poppy's
grandparents.

"Follow your dreams!"
said Poppy's mother
and father.

"And remember, we'll be with you
every step of the way."

"Here's a little something for good luck," said Emma. She handed Poppy a good luck charm. "It's a big world, little pig, but remember that everyone smiles in the same language!" Poppy smiled, and then it was time to go!

When Poppy arrived at the World Athlete Village, she saw so many different athletes from all over the world. Would they speak the same language? Would she make any new friends?

The village was so big. How
would she find her way around?
Poppy felt very nervous.

Poppy had to find the check-in booth,

but she didn't know where to go!

She was so nervous she accidentally bumped

into a snowboarder from China named Li.

"Do you know where the check-in booth is?" Poppy asked.

Li said, "I have a map! Let's find it together!"

They talked and talked as they walked around the

Athlete Village. They even taught each other

a few words in their own languages.

"Hello" and "Ni hao" they said to each other.

As they waited in line at the check-in booth,

Poppy showed Li her good luck charm.

"Cool," said Li. "I have a lucky charm too!"

And he showed Poppy his jade goldfish.

Poppy smiled at her new friend
and her new friend smiled back.
Emma was right! They both
smiled in the same language.
Poppy started to feel a little
better about her adventure
in Paris. Poppy and Li
wished each other good
luck in the competition
and waved good-bye.

Poppy was soon very hungry and decided to eat in the athletes' dining hall. She looked around the crowded room for a friendly face.

A skier from Italy named Gianna waved and offered Poppy a spot at her table. "Do you like Italian food? We can share!" Gianna said.

"It's my favorite!" said Poppy. "From pasta to gelato…and of course pizza!"

Poppy and Gianna talked and talked about food and music and discovered how much they both loved Poochini, an Italian composer!

Poppy smiled at her new friend
and her new friend smiled back.
"Buona fortuna!" they said,
wishing each other good luck.

It was time for Poppy to go to practice. She was dressed in her competition costume and was a little worried it might be too different.

Another ice-skater was standing near Poppy. She was from Japan and her name was Kiyomi.

Kiyomi was dressed in
her competition costume too.
It was like nothing Poppy
had ever seen!

Poppy admired Kiyomi's bold
and brightly colored dress.
Kiyomi looked at Poppy's
spectacular sparkly dress.
"I like your costume!" they
said at the same time.

Poppy and Kiyomi discovered they both loved fashion and designed their own costumes. "I dream of being a fabulous fashion designer," said Kiyomi. Poppy knew all about dreams too!

Poppy smiled at her new friend
and her new friend smiled back.
"Ganbatte kudasai" they said,
wishing each other good luck.

It was time for the competition to start. Poppy waited backstage and thought about how wonderful it was to have met so many new friends. Just then she saw a speed skater from Australia named Zoe. She looked very scared and nervous. Poppy knew just how she felt.

"When I'm nervous," Poppy told Zoe, "I think about what my grandparents and best friend always tell me. They cheer 'dream big' and 'you go, girl!'"

"Thanks," said Zoe. "My friends and family always tell me 'you can do it!'"

Poppy and Zoe talked and talked about
how much their family and friends support
them and love them no matter what!

Poppy smiled at her new friend
and her new friend smiled back.
Zoe wasn't nervous anymore
because she had made a new
friend in Poppy!
They wished each other good
luck and said "hooroo!" which
means good-bye.

Poppy took to the ice. She felt the joy
of new friendships and discoveries.
She skated from her heart.
She knew she would always
remember this special trip.

When Poppy skated off the ice, her mother and father gave her a huge hug. They were so proud of her.

"I'm so happy you traveled so far!" her father said.

"I'm so happy you followed your dreams!" her mother said.

In celebration, Poppy and her family spent
the rest of the week in Paris, the City of Lights! They
saw the Eiffel Tower and visited art museums.
They even ate some French food.

Poppy bought four postcards. She addressed them to Li the snowboarder, Gianna the skier, Kiyomi the ice skater, and Zoe the speed skater.

"I'm so glad we became friends!" she wrote.
"Even though we are from different parts of the
big world, we all smile in the same language!"
And then she signed each postcard,

Love, Poppy ☺

About the Author

Kristi Yamaguchi is an Olympic figure skating champion, winner of *Dancing with the Stars*, and *New York Times* bestselling author of *Dream Big, Little Pig*. Her motto "Always Dream" contributed to her success on and off the ice and is one that she aspires to instill in the hearts of children. Kristi currently lives in the San Francisco Bay Area with her husband and their two young daughters.

This is dedicated to all of the children in our Big World. *Always dream and keep smiling!*

Love, Kristi

To my friend, Lorraine Merriman Farrell
—T.B.

Acknowledgments

Thank you to the incredible team at Sourcebooks for all you do! Tim Bowers for bringing the pages to life. And Yuki Saegusa for your guidance, support, and most of all, friendship through the years. My heartfelt thanks to you all!

—Kristi

A portion of Kristi's proceeds from this book will benefit the Always Dream Foundation.

Visit her at
www.alwaysdream.org.

About the Illustrator

New York Times bestselling illustrator Tim Bowers has always had a love for animals. In fact, he enjoyed spending time at his grandparents' home visiting their furry friends, which at one time included a pet pig named Porky! Tim has illustrated more than twenty-five children's books and received numerous awards for his delightfully sweet and silly illustrations. He often visits schools to promote literacy and to share his experience and love for illustrating children's books. Tim Bowers lives in Ohio with his wife.

Visit him at
www.timbowers.com.